Kittymouse

Kittymouse

Sumiko

Harcourt Brace Jovanovich   New York and London

One day a mouse family found a kitten in their nest.

"Why, she's just a baby!" cried Mrs Mouse. "Poor little thing, she's all alone. We must look after her and give her a good home."

"Kittens grow into cats, my dear," said Mr Mouse. "Is it wise?"

"We'll bring her up to be a mouse," said Mrs Mouse firmly. "There won't be any trouble."

Tilly, Milly and Max were delighted with
their new sister. They called her Kittymouse.
They taught her how to squeak and showed
her how to nibble nuts and acorns.

At night they all curled up together in a
cosy ball.

As soon as Kittymouse was big
enough, she would roam the streets
with Mr Mouse, picking up scraps
of food for the family.

It was always hard to find enough
for them all.

"Kittymouse eats so much more than the others," Mrs Mouse complained. "The poor child is always hungry."

"Why don't we find a nice house to live in, with a kitchen full of crumbs?" suggested Mr Mouse. "I'm sick and tired of poking about in the open. I know the very place for us."

The family moved in without delay.

They found a perfect hiding place in the
cellar. Mr Mouse hurried up to the kitchen to
get some food and came back triumphantly
with the finest meal they had ever seen.

Kittymouse gazed hungrily at the delicious
titbits.

"May we go up to the kitchen too?" she asked.
"Your father and I will have a good look
round, and if it is safe we will show you the
whole house," said Mrs Mouse. "But you must
promise to be very careful. There is a cat in this
house. I can smell it!"

Next day Mrs Mouse showed the children where it was safe for them to play, and where all the mouseholes were, so that they could escape if the cat came near.

Tilly, Milly and Max scampered all over the furniture and played hide-and-seek in some old shoes, while Kittymouse chased balls of crumpled paper from the wastepaper basket. They had a wonderful time.

"Time to go home," called Mrs Mouse at last. "You may play again tomorrow, but you must on no account go near that mousetrap. And you must *always* keep away from the cat. Do you understand?"

Everyone nodded seriously except Kittymouse.

Tilly, Milly and Max soon learned to scamper about the house without being seen, and to pick up delicious scraps to eat.

But Kittymouse was not so clever at hiding. And she had big, clumsy paws that could not pick up tiny crumbs.

"She is getting bigger every day," said Mrs Mouse anxiously to her husband. "We can't let her run around with the others – she'll be seen. We shall have to bring her food in the cellar."

Kittymouse got bigger still.

It was dull for Kittymouse in the cellar. She wanted to romp round the kitchen with her brother and sisters. She disobeyed Mrs Mouse, and ran upstairs when she wasn't looking.

One day, they were playing on the kitchen shelves when a big white cat came in. They all shot out of sight.

"Meow!" said the cat.

"Meow!" said Kittymouse, from behind the marmalade pot. She *was* surprised. She had been squeaking all her life, and here she was making a sound like the cat.

"Meow!" Kittymouse said again. The white cat stalked round and round the kitchen while Tilly, Milly, Max and Kittymouse kept quite still.

Then he stalked out again.

After that Kittymouse got bolder and bolder. She liked poking about the house, and she wasn't going to stay hidden, whatever Mrs Mouse said.

One day, Kittymouse was playing in the wastepaper basket when a dreadful thing happened.

"Look – a kitten!" cried a voice, and a hand reached towards her. Kittymouse leapt out of the basket, to see two children gazing down at her in surprise. She darted away.

"She's going down the mousehole!" said the girl.

"Perhaps she thinks she's a mouse," said her brother.

"We must put out some milk for her," said the little girl. "Then she might come up and play with us."

But Kittymouse was well away, down in the cellar.

"I told you to be careful!" scolded Mrs Mouse. "You keep away from those children."

Kittymouse had had a fright – but she was curious.
She wanted to see the children again.

That night, when Mr and Mrs Mouse were fast
asleep, Max and Kittymouse crept upstairs to the
children's bedroom. Max was a bit frightened, but
Kittymouse never seemed to be afraid of anything.

"What's this?" said Kittymouse, sniffing at a bowl
that stood on the floor.

"Don't touch it, it's horrible! It's poison!" whispered
Max.

"Rubbish, it's delicious," she said. And she drank up
every single drop. It was her very first drink of milk.

Next day Kittymouse raced back upstairs. She wanted
some more of the delicious milk. And sure enough,
there on the floor was a bowl full of it.

Kittymouse was so busy lapping it up that she didn't
notice the door opening. Before she had time to run
away, she was scooped up in a pair of loving arms.

"Don't be afraid, kitty," said the little girl softly.
"You shall have your milk. We only want to play
with you."

To her surprise, Kittymouse was not afraid. She
liked the sound of the girl's gentle voice and the way
she tickled her furry tummy. She was warm and
comfortable. There was a queer sound rumbling up
inside her. For the first time in her life, Kittymouse
purred.

"Look in the mirror, kitty," whispered the little girl, " see what a beautiful pussy you are."

Kittymouse's eyes grew rounder and rounder. It was a cat! A strange, black cat staring at her from the glass. Poor Kittymouse was so frightened she jumped down and ran straight home to tell her mother.

"That wasn't another cat, it was your own reflection in the mirror," sighed Mrs Mouse. "I can see the time has come to tell you what you really are."

And she told Kittymouse how she had been found as a tiny kitten and brought up as a mouse.

"But I don't think you can be a mouse much longer," said Mrs Mouse sadly. "You'll soon be too big to get down a mousehole."

"Perhaps I could live upstairs," said Kittymouse. "Then I could have a bowl of milk every day. I'd like that."

So Kittymouse went to live with the two children, and they loved her just as much as the mouse family did, and gave her milk to drink and a toy mouse to play with.

But Kittymouse never forgot her first family. She visited them every day and invented wonderful games to play with her brother and sisters. She even made friends with the white cat and made sure he kept out of the kitchen when Mr Mouse was looking for food.

"I knew we'd be proud of our Kittymouse one day," said Mrs Mouse. "We need never fear the cat again."

And even when Kittymouse was quite grown up with four beautiful kittens of her own, she made sure they never did.

Copyright © 1976 by Gakken
This edition copyright © 1978 by Sumiko Davies
All rights reserved. No part of this publication may be reproduced or
transmitted in any form or by any means, electronic or mechanical, including
photocopy, recording, or any information storage and retrieval system,
without permission in writing from the publisher.
Idea and original story from Little Golden Book *The Kitten Who Thought
He Was A Mouse*, © Western Publishing Co. Inc., Racine, U.S.A., 1954
Printed in Great Britain

Library of Congress Cataloging in Publication Data

Sumiko.
Kittymouse.
Translation of Okashino neko no hanashi.
SUMMARY: Adopted as a kitten by a family of mice, a cat believes herself to be
a mouse until she comes in contact with two loving children.
[1. Cats—Fiction. 2. Mice—Fiction] I. Title.
PZ7.S9539Ki   [E]   78-16716
ISBN 0-15-243028-8

First American edition 1979

B C D E